BRISÉ

ENTRECHAT

PIROUETTE
À LA SECONDE

JETÉ

CABRIOLE

A Ladybird Book
Series 662

*Here is a book which will delight all who
have some interest in ballet. It will
also fascinate the general reader, and inspire
many to actually see a ballet in a theatre
and experience its excitement and enchantment.*

*The book tells the story of the development
of ballet from the early days of dancing
in the Royal Courts, explains the language
of ballet and classical mime and deals
with such subjects as styles of
dancing, training, clothes, shoes and
backstage preparations.*

*The last few pages describe and illustrate
such well-known ballets as* Giselle, Swan Lake,
The Sleeping Beauty, Les Sylphides *and others.*

A LADYBIRD BOOK

BALLET

by IAN WOODWARD
with illustrations by
MARTIN AITCHISON

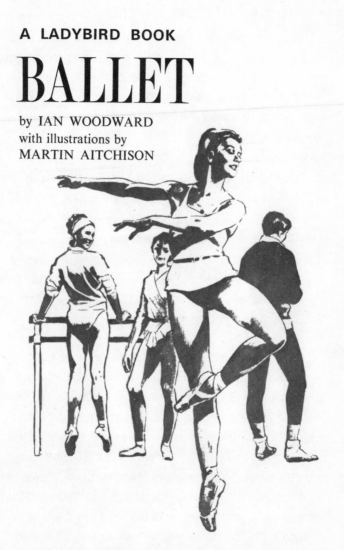

Publishers: Wills & Hepworth Ltd., Loughborough

First published 1969　　ⓒ　　*Printed in England*

Dancing in the Royal Courts

Who can fail to be excited by the sight of a pretty ballerina spinning across the stage? She represents everything we associate with lightness and grace. Her world has a special magic, too, where dancing, music and colourful scenery seem to conjure up a world of fantasy.

The ballet dancer developed gradually from the days when kings and queens loved to dance. The court 'spectacles', these were the earliest 'ballets', consisted of dancing, singing and long poetic speeches. There were no plots to these entertainments, merely a long series of charades. They began in Italy but soon spread to France, where Queen Catherine put them on a firm, artistic footing.

Towards the end of the sixteenth century, Catherine supervised the mounting of the first ballet with a dramatic plot, *Le Ballet Comique de la Reine*. In 1661, one of France's greatest dance-loving kings, Louis XIV, helped to continue the course of events by opening the first academy of dancing. Here all the steps introduced by the court ballet masters were codified, developed and passed on to future generations of dancers. Many of the steps you see in ballets like *Swan Lake* or *The Sleeping Beauty* can be traced back to Louis's academy.

An Italian court 'ballet' of the 15th century.

7214 0234 8

Dancing enters the Theatre

The court ballets were private affairs, and were often performed as much for the delight of those taking part as for those who watched. At first they took place in the great palace ballrooms and on magnificent lawns. Many of Louis XIV's ballets were seen in the royal stables. Later, a small theatre was built by his great-grandson, Louis XV, but admittance to it was by royal invitation only.

Quite soon, however, Paris was able to boast a few public theatres, and they proved very popular. At that time, only men appeared publicly, some wearing masks in imitation of women, who were banned from dancing on the stage. The ballets consisted of very simple steps. This was because the dancers were amateurs, and because the patterns formed by the positions of the dancers were considered more important than intricate footwork.

In the theatre, machinery and pulleys were used to create many marvellous effects. But this machinery, as well as the cumbersome clothes worn by the dancers, hindered any development of the ballet. Only after women became accepted at the Paris Opéra, in 1681, and Marie Camargo shortened her dancing dress a few inches in the 1720's, revealing her ankles, did the dancer begin to show that she could dazzle as an individual—well away from the geometric floor-patterns beloved by her predecessors.

The King of France attends a ballet performance in his private theatre.

Birth of the Romantic Ballet

When Camargo shortened her dress, and removed the heels from her shoes, she set the standard for a new type of dancer. Now, brilliant beats of the legs and amazing leaps took everyone's attention. Camargo had a great rival named Marie Sallé, who developed the dance even further. Sallé wore Greek muslin draperies and put emphasis on the interpretation and acting aspect rather on that of performing spectacular steps.

Meanwhile, Italy continued to produce great teachers like Blasis, Viganò, Angiolini, and Galeotti. Yet it was in Paris, at the Opéra, where ballet was to be seen at its best. In Copenhagen, too, towards the end of the eighteenth century, ballets of a notable standard were being produced by foreign ballet masters.

Until the beginning of the nineteenth century, ballets were either about everyday people, such as simple country folk, or about gods of antiquity, such as Apollo, Mars or Venus. But for about twenty years, between 1830 and 1850, people's imaginations were fired by romantic visions—of tales of fairies, gnomes, wilis and sylphides. This was the Romantic Period, which also affected painting, literature, drama, and music. It gave us dancers like Taglioni, Grahn, Elssler, Cerrito and Grisi, and the ballets *La Sylphide* and *Giselle* in Paris, and *Napoli* in Copenhagen.

8   *Marie Camargo dances in an early 18th century ballet.*

The influence of Russian Ballet

A few years before ballet became strongly influenced by Romanticism, one or two ballerinas practised the feat of dancing on the tips of their toes. However, this was inserted in a ballet merely as a gimmick. Afterwards, in 1832, Marie Taglioni introduced it in *La Sylphide*. Dancing on the toes immediately assumed a new meaning. It ideally created an impression of lightness, as though, in the form of a wili, or spirit of the night, the ballerina was ready to take off in flight.

The ballerina was idolised during the Romantic Period, and the ballets were notable for contrasting the real with the unreal: village maidens figured opposite supernatural beings. *Giselle*, produced in 1841, is one of the most popular ballets still being performed that stems from this period.

Paris's contribution to ballet faded during the second half of the nineteenth century, although one or two notable ballets appeared, such as *Coppélia* and *The Two Pigeons*. But it was in Russia, at the Maryinsky Theatre in St. Petersburg, where attention on ballet was now being focussed. There the great Tchaikovsky ballets were created: *The Sleeping Beauty*, *The Nutcracker* and *Swan Lake*.

From Russia, too, came a man named Serge Diaghilev, who brought many great dancers, composers, choreographers, and painters to Europe. Pavlova, Karsavina and Nijinsky were among them. These dancers, and the ballets they appeared in, like *Petrouchka* and *Les Sylphides*, had a profound influence, particularly in England.

10   *Anna Pavlova dances her famous solo, 'The Dying Swan'.*

History before our Eyes

When you watch *The Sleeping Beauty*, or any other ballet, you are seeing little touches of history. When we say a dancer is 'graceful', we actually mean that the head, arms and hands are correctly 'placed' in the style of a court dancer in seventeenth-century France. All courtiers were proficient swordsmen. Their movements were circular and harmonious, and their legs were turned out to help movement in any direction. Arms and hands were forced into a curved position by the continual lifting of heavy costumes.

We are now ready for a definition of the word 'ballet'. It means more than simply dancers dancing. That is just a part of our description. There is also the music, the choreography (the art of dance creation), and the décor (or scenery and costumes). When these are mixed by an expert, they can produce a beautiful ballet—perhaps a classic.

So when you go to the ballet, try to be appreciative of its history, and of the people who are today carrying on its tradition. Read the story of the ballet before the performance, and ask someone to explain any queries before the lights are dimmed. You can then give the performance all the careful attention it deserves. If a solo gives you particular enjoyment, do not be afraid to clap at the end of it. This is the only way we have to say 'Thank you'.

Dancing + drama + décor + music = ballet.

Dancing + drama + dé

DANCING
+
DRAMA
+
DÉCOR
+
MUSIC

EQUALS
BALLET

Understanding the Language (1)

We have seen that ballet grew up in the French court, and this is why most of the terms used to describe dance steps and movements are in the French language. Dancers begin and end all steps in one of the Five Positions of the Feet. These help the body to be properly balanced in almost any position. You will see, from the illustrations in the end-papers of this book, that in every position the legs are fully 'turned-out'. There are various positions for the arms, too.

If you watched a ballet class, you would see that the dancers begin by doing *pliés* at the *barre*. A *plié* is a bending of the knees, with the legs in a fully turned-out position. It helps to loosen the muscles and develop balance. The *barre*, or rail, is held gently by the dancer as a form of support.

Away from the *barre*, a dancer may perform a spinning movement, with one foot *sur la pointe* (on the tip of the toe) and the other on the knee-cap. This is a *pirouette*. Or she may 'glide' across the floor, her feet moving in small, rapid steps. She would be doing *pas de bourrées*, which is a step used by Myrtha on her first entrance in *Giselle*. The word *pas* means step or dance. A *pas de deux* is a dance for two, *de trois* for three, and so on.

14   *Ballet class—a dancer practises a 'spin' or pirouette.*

Understanding the Language (2)

If a number of steps are put together, thus forming a little dance, it is known as an *enchaînement* (which means 'linking'). Another word you will come across is *divertissement*. This refers to a number of 'show-piece' dances inserted in a ballet and usually bearing no relation to the story. The last act of *The Nutcracker* is really one long *divertissement*.

A dancer with good *elevation* is one who jumps high and lands softly. He might also have good *ballon*, when he seems to bounce into the air like a ball when his feet touch the ground after a jump. Some dancers more easily perform steps in the air (*en l'air*), while others are best suited to *terre à terre* (ground to ground) dancing.

One of the highlights of a classical ballet is the *adagio*—the Rose Adagio in *The Sleeping Beauty* is a supreme example. Here the ballerina, supported by the *premier danseur* (her male equivalent) displays to advantage her line and technique. The whole dance is performed very leisurely. *Allegro* is the opposite: brisk and lively. *Allegro* exercises come near the end of every class.

You will find illustrations of several ballet steps on the front and back endpapers of this book.

Elevation—the ability to jump high and land softly.

The Ballet Student

Any boy or girl who wants to take up ballet training with a view to pursuing the dance as a profession, must possess a suitable physique and good health. Eight or nine is the best age to begin. Britain's Royal Ballet, the Royal Danish Ballet, the Paris Opéra Ballet, and all the leading schools in Russia accept pupils at nine or ten.

If the young student starts too early, her bones will still be soft and if she starts too late the muscles and tendons will have stiffened. To possess a good turn-out of the legs, where the feet and legs turn out *from the hip*, preparatory lessons at the recommended minimum age are necessary. Girls should not start *pointe* work until they are eleven or twelve.

For the first year, two lessons a week are advised, with perhaps half an hour of private instruction once a month. The serious student must eventually take daily classes, particularly if she hopes to be successful in her examinations. Besides the obvious work at the *barre* and other exercises in the centre of the classroom, a working knowledge of music will prove a great help. There is a lot to be learned in ballet, which is why the general training usually lasts up to the seventeenth or eighteenth birthday.

Top—young dancers at the barre.
Bottom—students in the 'attitude' position.

Exercises and Rehearsals

A large part of the dancer's day is taken up with rehearsals. Ballets in the current season, even well-known ones like *Coppélia* or *Les Sylphides*, must be continually rehearsed by the dancers. There are always dancers away sick, and other dancers who must be taught their roles. Dancers new to the company also have to learn each ballet in the repertory as it is scheduled for performance. Precision in the *corps de ballet* is most important. To achieve this, the ballet master will spend many hours rehearsing his dancers.

Ocasionally, new ballets have to be learned. Here the dancers may even influence the finished 'shape' of the ballet. The man who creates the new ballets is the *choreographer*. This word stems from two Greek words, meaning 'writer' or 'creator of dances'.

If you were to visit a rehearsal studio, you would probably find all four walls flanked by huge mirrors and surrounded by a *barre*. All dancers must have at least one and a quarter hours of exercises every day of their working lives. These exercises keep their muscles supple and their joints flexible. The mirrors are there so that the dancer can see exactly what her body, legs and arms are doing. That, in short, their poses and movements are beautiful to the eye.

A ballet master takes a rehearsal.

Creating a New Ballet

An important role of any ballet company is to create new works. While a few companies can rely on established works from the past to fill their repertories, the dance can only develop and enrich itself if there is a continual flow of new ballets being produced. What is more, it is the thing dancers enjoy doing most—being 'in' on everything from the very beginning.

The initial idea for a new ballet usually comes from the choreographer himself. If the ballet is to be without a plot, then the choreographer will probably know exactly what he wants. But if there is to be a definite story, such as one based on the life of Joan of Arc, then he may call in the help of a scenarist (person who writes the story) so that the work has a proper dramatic interest.

Teamwork and close collaboration is essential. If existing music is not being used, then a score will have to be commissioned. A designer, too, is needed. Each must know what the others want before a single step is danced. However, many things—rhythm of the music, length of the dresses, duration of a solo—may be altered in the course of creation, for this is how ballets are made.

The designer explains a point to the choreographer.

Styles of Dancing

In ballet we find 'lyrical' dancers, possessing soft, free-flowing movements; and 'musical' dancers, who respond naturally to the general 'feel' of the music; and virtuoso (or 'fireworks') dancers, who excel at difficult technical steps. We also find 'cold', 'warm' or 'hard' dancers, depending on their own personalities and the training they have received. Or a dancer may shine in comedy roles, when she will be known as a *soubrette*.

All these qualities determine the type of dancers they are, and the sort of roles to which they are suited. As a rule, dancers fall into five general 'styles': classical, semi-character, character, national, and mime. The classical dancer relies entirely on a perfect technique, calling for very little character-building (example: Princess Aurora in *The Sleeping Beauty*). A classical technique is also used by the semi-character dancer, but the style also calls for a fair amount of acting (example: Lise in *La Fille mal Gardée*).

A dancer taking a character part must be a very good actor, for he will usually be portraying a character entirely different to his real self (example: Rothbart in *Swan Lake*). Mime roles require no dancing at all, although they may play an important part in the ballet (example: Dr. Coppélius in *Coppélia*). Dances of various countries are given to the national dancer (example: The Russian Dancers in *The Nutcracker*).

Types of dancers—1. *classical*; 2. *semi-character*; 3. *character*; 4. *mime*; 5. *national*.

Classical Mime

In new ballets with a modern story, gestures (based on natural movements) are used to express actions and feelings. These gestures may be elaborations of the natural movements, being what we call 'stylized'.

However, in the surviving classical ballets, mime is used instead. This provides the dancers with a means of conveying to the audience what he is 'saying' or what he is trying to convey to another dancer on the stage. With mime, the face, limbs and body act as his 'mouth'.

One of the most important influences in the history of mime was the *Commedia dell'Arte* (which means 'Italian improvised comedy'), when little troupes of actors and dancers travelled Italy and Europe three hundred years ago. Through the years, they devised a form of mime that could be readily understood by peoples of any nationality. These troupes often performed in the French courts—and so, eventually, mime reached ballet. Much of the mime, however, is based on a deaf and dumb language invented in the eighteenth century. Many of these signs, as used in the classical ballets, are little understood today by the average balletgoer.

The use of 'mime' in ballet.

ME   YOU   LOVE   TEARS

ANGER   HIDE   1 - DEATH - 2

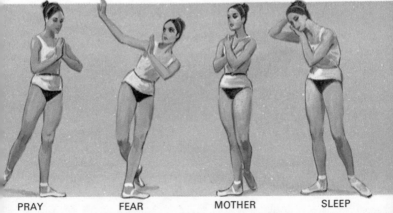

PRAY   FEAR   MOTHER   SLEEP

Dancing on the Toes

Dancing on the tips of the toes—*sur les pointes*—is what distinguishes the classical ballerina from any other type of dancer in the theatre. It is not so painful nor as difficult as it looks, although the student has to contend with aching and bleeding toes until she masters the art. During Taglioni's time, the ballerinas used normal soft cloth shoes, padded with cotton wool, for *pointe* work. Gradually, it was found that more comfortable support could be obtained by stiffening the toe-end of the shoe with glue. What resulted was the 'blocked' shoe.

Dancers select their shoes very carefully indeed, for an ill-fitting pair could cause untold damage to their feet. The blocks, for instance, must provide adequate support while at the same time allowing the dancer to 'feel' the floor. The reinforced sole must also have just the right amount of springiness. It must be neither too stiff nor too soft.

The dancer always sews her own ribbons on her shoes. She also darns the tip of her *pointe* shoes to prolong their life and to provide extra 'cushion' and 'grip'. This is because ballet shoes are very short-lived. Svetlana Beriosova, for example, may use three pairs in a full-length ballet like *The Sleeping Beauty*.

Top, left—dancing 'sur les pointes'.
Top, right—the 'blocked' shoe.
Below—dancer darning her pointed shoes.

Tutus, Tights and Leotards

All ballet dancers wear cotton, silk or nylon tights, with briefs underneath. These are thought to have come into general practice at the end of the eighteenth century, so that the legs would be covered when the skirts became shorter. Tights worn in the classroom are usually made of wool, so that the leg muscles are kept warm during periods of non-activity. Sometimes a *leotard* is worn over the tights. This resembles a one-piece bathing-suit, with or without sleeves.

Basically, there are two kinds of ballet dress. The oldest is the bell-shaped Romantic dress (or tutu), which Taglioni popularised in *La Sylphide* and which Michel Fokine utilised in his *Les Sylphides* earlier this century. It is made from many layers of fine tulle and reaches midway between the knee and the ankle. The classical tutu, the second type of dress, is perhaps the most familiar. The word tutu means skirt, and the classical tutu is extremely short and stiff. Layers and layers of tarlatan frills make it project outwards.

All ballet dresses reflect the nature of the ballets in which they appear. The classical tutu provides ample freedom of movement for virtuoso dancing. On the other hand, poetic, lyrical dancing befits the Romantic dress.

Left—sleeveless leotard worn over tights.
Top, right—the classical tutu.
Lower, right—the Romantic dress.

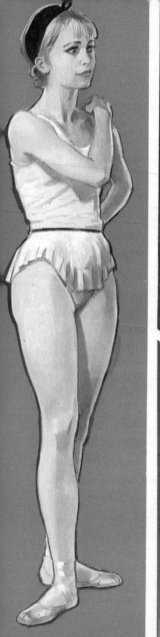

The Purpose of Make-up

If you were to be invited round to a dancer's dressing room after a performance, you would soon notice her stage make-up. Her face would be laden with grease-paint and powder, and every feature—eyes, nose, mouth, cheeks, chin—would be 'made-up' to suit either the characteristics of the dancer or the part she has been portraying.

The eyes receive special attention, because they are so important to the dancer in expressing various emotions, like happiness, sadness, anger, and so on. But if her eyes and other facial characteristics are to be seen at all clearly by people sitting a long way off in the audience, then these must be highlighted—which means exaggerating them—to make any effect. Make-up is also used to counteract the glare of the brilliant stage lighting.

You will see in the illustration how the dancer's eyes have been extended by line pencils, and the eyebrows raised slightly with black mascara. A foundation is first applied over the whole face, followed by shadows and highlights. Next the cheeks and lips are coloured with rouge, finishing off by making-up the eyes. Make-up must also be applied to all parts of the skin that are visible—neck, arms and hands—otherwise they appear ghostly white.

The dancer 'makes-up' her face.
Below—notice the attention given to the eyes.

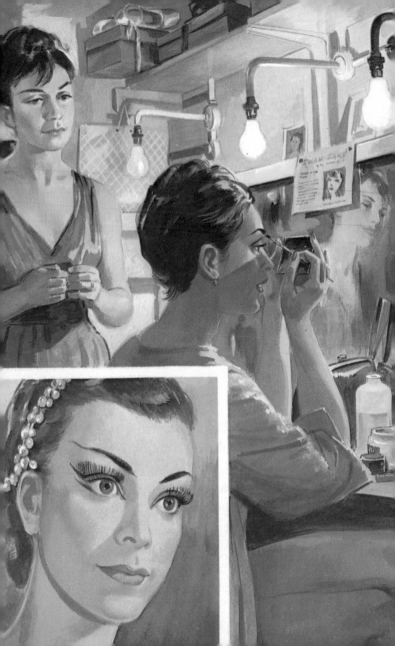

Backstage Excitement

In the dressing rooms, dancers are making-up and changing into their costumes for the next performance. Over the loudspeaker, in one corner of the room, a voice announces 'Overture and beginners on stage, please!' Some of the dancers are ready, and others are still fixing their hair or tightening their bodices as they scuttle away towards the stage.

It seems difficult to imagine, with all the bustle and chaos backstage at this particular moment, that a ballet is about to be performed. Someone notices that a piece of scenery is not where it should be. Some stagehands make some final adjustments. One of the carpenters is busy at the back of the stage. There is a frantic call of 'Lower these lights, Harry.'

The overture is still being played as some of the dancers warm-up by doing *pliés*, or kick their legs sharply into the air. Some dancers practise a spin or two, while others dip their feet into a box of rosin to give their shoes added 'grip'. A man in a grey suit, the ballet master, is chatting to a couple of the principal dancers. Suddenly a voice orders everyone to take their correct places. All is tense. At last, up goes the curtain for another two or three hours of magic and make-believe.

Backstage—just before 'curtain-up'.

Bowing and Curtseying

At the end of a ballet, or when an important solo has just been danced, the ballerina will invariably acknowledge the applause by taking a 'call'. This takes the form of a bow or curtsey. The way the 'call' is taken varies according to the role being danced. It also depends on the dancer, for every ballerina has her own particular way of curtseying, and the elaborate displays often seen are performances in their own right.

Generally speaking, however, we can say that there are two ways to take a call—the Romantic curtsey, and the classical bow. The male dancer usually bows, and, when taking a call with the ballerina, is often given a flower by her as a gesture of appreciation. The curtsey comes direct to us from the courts of seventeenth-century France. The bow was first performed by a female dancer in 1886, when an Italian ballerina introduced it to the Maryinsky Theatre in St. Petersburg.

The wonderful bouquets and baskets of flowers you see presented to the ballerina at the end of the performance invariably come from friends and admirers, or perhaps from a well-wisher in her own company. She never sends herself flowers. Occasionally, the male dancer may receive a laurel wreath.

Stage-call—the classical bow and curtsey.

'La Sylphide'

The audience who flocked to the Paris Opéra on 12th March, 1832, for the first performance of Filippo Taglioni's *La Sylphide*, witnessed a new era in the history of dance—the Romantic Ballet. For the next twenty years, ballets were based on stories featuring the real and ethereal. *La Sylphide* has a Scottish setting and tells of James who falls in love with a Sylphide. But, being of another world, she is unattainable, and finally dies in James's arms. Marie Taglioni, in the title-role, scored her greatest triumph. Her long bell-shaped dress was to become accepted as the typical Romantic dress.

'Giselle'

The Romantic Period was at its height when *Giselle* was first produced in Paris in 1841. Like *La Sylphide*, the first act concerns human beings, the second with wilis of the forest. Giselle is a pretty peasant girl who is in love with Albrecht. When she discovers that he is really a prince, and already engaged to someone else, she loses her reason and stabs herself. In the second act, we see Giselle as a wili. She appears briefly before Albrecht, now heart-broken, only to return to her grave as dawn approaches. The ballet has lovely music by Adolphe Adam, and the central role is considered to be the Hamlet of the dance.

Above—a scene from 'La Sylphide'.
Below—a scene from 'Giselle'.

'Swan Lake'

In this ballet, Princess Odette has been turned into a swan by an evil magician, and can only assume human form for ever by a man's faithful love. Prince Siegfried is in love with her. When the magician realises this he transforms his daughter, Odile, into a faithful image of Odette. Siegfried, fooled by the disguise, swears his love for Odile. When he discovers his mistake, Siegfried and Odette throw themselves into the lake. There they find eternal love.

Romanticism in ballet had been dead for over twenty years when *Swan Lake* was mounted at the Bolshoi Theatre, Moscow, in 1877. The choice of a Romantic theme, therefore, was perhaps a little odd, although its initial failure had nothing to do with the theme. Nor was Tchaikovsky's music to blame, although it was a great advance on the customary music of that time. A mediocre choreographer, an amateur conductor, poor costumes and scenery, all helped to make *Swan Lake* a complete fiasco.

Many years later it was revived by Marius Petipa and his assistant, Lev Ivanov, and first performed in four acts at the Maryinsky Theatre, St. Petersburg, in 1895. It is this version which survives today. The dual role of Odette-Odile is a great test for the ballerina. It calls for lyricism, warmth and tenderness in the one role, and, in the other, for virtuosity and a sense of drama and evil forboding.

Siegfried and Odile, and the evil magician, are confronted by the vision of Odette in 'Swan Lake'.

'The Sleeping Beauty'

The Sleeping Beauty is based on a famous story by Charles Perrault, and is the result of close collaboration between Petipa, the choreographer, and Tchaikovsky, the composer. Its choreography and music has now become associated with everything that is grand and magnificent in Russian Ballet. The ballerina role is pure classicism, demanding dignity, purity of line, and an abundance of artistry. There are, too, various opportunities for soloists in fairy roles, and for the famous Blue Birds. Since the first performance in 1890 at the Maryinsky Theatre, St. Petersburg, the ballet has known surprisingly few really great Auroras. Among the exceptions have been Margot Fonteyn in England and Irina Kolpakova in Russia.

'The Nutcracker'

The Dance of the Sugar-Plum Fairy must be one of the most popular pieces of ballet music. It comes from Tchaikovsky's The Nutcracker, and the unmistakable 'sound' is produced by a small keyboard instrument called a celesta. Petipa also planned this ballet, but he fell ill and handed over the job of choreography to Ivanov. The story is about a little girl named Clara whose Christmas present, a huge nutcracker, turns into a Prince and takes her on a trip to the Kingdom of the Sweets. It was first performed at the Maryinsky Theatre in 1892. The first full-length version in England was mounted in 1934 for the Vic-Wells Ballets, with Alicia Markova as the Fairy.

Above—Princess Aurora and the Prince, with one of the two Blue Birds, in 'The Sleeping Beauty'. Below—The Sugar-Plum Fairy and the Prince, with the Russian Dancers, in 'The Nutcracker'.

42

'Coppelia'

Coppélia is based on a story by Hoffmann and was first performed at the Paris Opéra in 1870. The choreography is by Arthur Saint-Léon, and it has music by Leo Delibes. Four years earlier, Delibes had collaborated with Minkus in writing the score for *La Source*. But *Coppélia* was his first full-length ballet, which, with *Sylvia* in 1876, soon established him as one of the greatest composers in this art-form.

Unlike Romantic Ballet, *Coppélia* was about everyday people, and it became an instant success. The role of Franz was at one time danced by a girl at the Paris Opéra. Different versions of the ballet are to be seen all over the world. The Royal Danish Ballet have been dancing it since 1896.

Coppélia is often to be seen sitting at the window of the mysterious Dr. Coppélius's workshop. Franz has fallen in love with her, not knowing that she is really a doll. Swanilda, his fiancée, becomes jealous of Coppélia. Presently, Swanilda and her friends creep into Dr. Coppélius's workshop, discover Coppélia is only a doll, and play a prank on the old man by setting in motion all the clockwork puppets in the room. In the end, Franz and Swanilda are reconciled, and the entire town is enjoying the wedding celebrations as the curtain comes down.

Swanilda and her friends creep into Dr. Coppélius's workshop—from 'Coppélia.'

'Les Sylphides'

This beautiful ballet by Fokine, with music by Chopin, should not be confused with *La Sylphide*, although both are similar in spirit. Fokine wanted to create a ballet that would evoke the Romanticism of Marie Taglioni. This is why all the dancers (there is only one male dancer) wear the famous white bell-shaped dress, with a band of tiny rosebuds in the hair. *Les Sylphides* was first performed in Paris in 1909 by Diaghilev's Ballets Russes, with a cast headed by Pavlova, Karsavina and Nijinsky. There is no story to the ballet, but the male dancer is often said to be a poet who sees the sylphides around him as fleeting visions of his own creative thought.

'Petrouchka'

Petrouchka, with choreography by Fokine, music by Stravinsky, and décor by Benois, is one of the greatest dance-dramas in the world repertory. It is also a perfect example of the unity which can result when choreographer, librettist, composer and designer get together to collaborate on equal terms. The ballet, in four scenes, is set in the middle of a noisy Russian fair. The principal characters are three puppets—Petrouchka and the Moor, who are both in love with the Ballerina. Nijinsky immortalised the role of Petrouchka, and Karsavina was the original Ballerina. The ballet was first performed by Diaghilev's company in 1911.

Two Fokine ballets: above—the poet and ensemble in 'Les Sylphides'; below—Ballerina, Petrouchka, and the Moor in 'Petrouchka'.

'Checkmate'

If you play chess, you will have no trouble following this one-act dance-drama by Ninette de Valois. With a dramatic score by Arthur Bliss, *Checkmate* is a ballet about Love and Death. The story is told symbolically, with a huge chessboard as the setting, and the people in the story are named after the pieces used in a game of chess. So there are Kings and Queens, Knights and Castles, Bishops and Pawns. When the ballet begins, they are half puppet and half human. Gradually they assume their own identities, with very real emotions. *Checkmate* was first performed in Paris in 1937 by the Sadler's Wells (now Royal) Ballet.

'Serenade'

George Balanchine left his native Russia in 1933 and went to America. He has lived there ever since and is one of today's greatest choreographers. When he first arrived there, he formed the School of American Ballet, and it was for his students that he created *Serenade* in 1934. Today it is a classic almost on a par with *Les Sylphides*. Like so many of Balanchine's ballets, it has no story. The dancers merely interpret the various moods suggested by Tchaikovsky's music, the Serenade in C for Strings. It is performed today by the New York City Ballet, the Royal Ballet, and many other companies.

Scenes from, above—de Valois's 'Checkmate'
below—Balanchine's 'Serenade'.

'Cinderella'

Like *The Sleeping Beauty*, *Cinderella* is based on a fairy-tale by Perrault. There have been many versions of this ballet during the last hundred years or so. Petipa, Cecchetti and Ivanov mounted a version in 1893 at the Maryinsky Theatre. But the most notable productions today are those with music by the Russian composer Serge Prokofiev. The three major productions are those by Frederick Ashton for the Royal Ballet, Rostislav Zakharov for the Bolshoi Ballet, and Konstantin Sergeyev for the Kirov Ballet. Famous Cinderellas have been Moira Shearer and Margot Fonteyn in England, and Galina Ulanova in Russia. Few ballets conjure up more of a fairy-tale atmosphere than this.

'La Fille mal Gardée'

The literal translation of this two-act ballet is 'The Girl Badly Treated'. It was first danced in Bordeaux in 1786, which makes it the oldest ballet still being performed by companies all over the world. The original choreography was by Jean Dauberval, with music by various composers. The story is of a girl named Lise, whose mother tries to marry her off to a rich simpleton named Alain. But Lise outwits her mother and finally marries Colas, the boy she really loves. There have been a number of scores written for this ballet, but Ashton chose the one by Ferdinand Hérold (1828) when he staged his version for the Royal Ballet in 1960.

Above—scene from Prokofiev's 'Cinderella'.
Below—Widow Simone, Alain, Colas and Lise
in Ashton's 'La Fille mal Gardée'.

THE FIVE POSITIONS OF THE FEET AND ARMS

1st 2nd 3rd 4th 5th

PLIÉS AT
THE BARRE

ARABESQUE

ATTITUDE

FOUETTÉ
(Basic leg and arm positions)